The Cowardly Lion

First published in 2010
by Wayland

This paperback edition published in 2014 by Wayland
Published under a different series title in hardback

Wayland
338 Euston Road
London NW1 3BH

Wayland Australia
Level 17/207 Kent Street
Sydney, NSW 2000

Series Editor: Louise John
Editor: Katie Powell
Cover design: Paul Cherrill
Design: D.R.ink
Consultant: Shirley Bickler

A CIP catalogue record for this book is available from the British Library.

ISBN 9780750266055

Printed in China

Wayland is a division of Hachette Children's Books,
an Hachette UK Company

www.hachette.co.uk

3 5 7 9 10 8 6 4

The Cowardly Lion

Written by Joe Hackett
Illustrated by Mike Spoor

WAYLAND

Latif the lion was having yet another hard day at Animal School.

Latif was a very cowardly sort of lion.
Everything seemed to scare him.

He hid behind trees and he never **ever** growled, let alone roared.

Suddenly, there was a loud noise
at the back of the classroom.

Latif fell off his chair with fright.
"What on earth was that?" he yelped.

But it was only Robert the rhino
dropping a book.

CRASH!

"Calm down," said Robert. "I thought
lions were supposed to be brave
and strong."

Twitcher the rabbit sat next to Latif and wagged her ears up and down.

"Please don't do that. It makes me jittery," Latif pleaded.

Then, Toby the terrier, at the back of the class, started to bark.

Latif put his paws over his ears and whimpered, "Stop it! You're scaring me!"

Finally, Finlay the frog jumped across the classroom, from one desk to another, and landed right in Latif's lap. It was the last straw.

"Waaah!" yowled Latif. He was so scared that **he** jumped straight into the arms of the teacher, Mrs Hooper.

"What are we going to do with you, Latif?" she said kindly. "You're a bundle of nerves. I thought lions were supposed to be brave and strong."

"Not me," Latif said sadly. "I'm a rather cowardly lion."

Later, at playtime, Latif's friends decided to help him. Enough was enough.

"I'll suddenly hoot very loudly," said Oliver the owl. "Then you can roar at the top of your voice and scare me away."

"I'm not really sure," replied Latif, timidly. "You're very kind, but I don't see how this is going to help..."

"Twit-twooooooo!" shouted
Oliver, suddenly.

Latif jumped out of his skin.
Then, he let out a tiny little growl.

"That's no good! Louder!" boomed
Oliver. So, Latif roared a little
bit louder.

"Better," nodded Oliver.

Tessie the tortoise was next.
"I'll pretend to fight with you,"
she said. "You must puff up your
mane and show me your claws."

Latif looked a bit worried.
"Come on then, show us what you're
made of!" shouted Tessie, as she bopped
him on the nose.

Latif took a deep breath, growled,
and bared his claws.

"Well done," said Tessie.
"You almost look scary."

"Do I?" asked Latif. "Really?"

"Now I'm going to tease you until you get really cross and show us your teeth," said Patty the pig.

She started calling him names and poking him with a stick.

"Scaredy cat, scaredy cat!"
taunted Patty.

"Don't be mean," whispered Latif,
and he started to walk away.

But Patty carried on. "You're a rubbish lion, with a rubbish roar!"

Latif stopped in his tracks.
Patty was being **really** mean.

"Stop it. I might bite you," he mumbled
under his breath.

"Say it again and show us you mean it," said Patty.

"STOP or I'll BITE you!" growled Latif, louder this time, and he bared his sharp white teeth at her.

Patty ran away. "Wow! You really scared me," she said.

Latif was extremely pleased
with himself.

He let out such a loud roar that all the other animals fled. Mrs Hooper came running out of the classroom.

"Goodness me, was that you, Latif?"
Mrs Hooper asked.

"It was indeed," boasted Latif, and smiled through his fierce whiskers. "Thanks to my friends, I'm a proper lion now!"

START READING is a series of highly enjoyable books for beginner readers. **The books have been carefully graded to match the Book Bands widely used in schools.** This enables readers to be sure they choose books that match their own reading ability.

Look out for the Band colour on the book in our Start Reading logo.

The Bands are:

Pink Band 1A & 1B

Red Band 2

Yellow Band 3

Blue Band 4

Green Band 5

Orange Band 6

Turquoise Band 7

Purple Band 8

Gold Band 9

START READING books can be read independently or shared with an adult. They promote the enjoyment of reading through satisfying stories supported by fun illustrations.

Joe Hackett was born on a farm. He remembers riding on a horse so big that he couldn't get his legs across its back. Now he lives on a little farm again, with his wife and dog Ozzie, who is small, black and brown, and loves best of all to go down badger and rabbit holes.

Mike Spoor loves being able to spend his days drawing the animals and pets of his childhood. He especially likes drawing animals with personalities that can be captured in his drawings, such as Latif the lion, Patty the pig, Finlay the frog and Tessie the tortoise.